T0304593

PLEASANT
FINDS

PLEASANT
FINDS

HENRI VENES

Library of Congress Control Number:		2012923844
ISBN:	Hardcover	978-1-4797-6903-2
	Softcover	978-1-4797-6902-5
	Ebook	978-1-4797-6904-9

To order additional copies of this book, contact:
Xlibris Corporation
1-888-795-4274
www.Xlibris.com
Orders@Xlibris.com
126737

This book is written and dedicated to Jennifer, my beautiful daughter, and Jason, my fearless son. Thank you both for the wonderful love, and support!

I

Moving to Washington State was the best thing she could have done. Lori had moved to Packwood from Virginia recently. It was just about a year now since she moved out west with her dog, Wilhelmina.

After living in the city of Virginia Beach, life out here was a welcome change. She could do without the everyday heavy traffic. Some days, while stuck in traffic for hours, she was able to plan what she would do differently if she could.

Packwood allowed Lori to live close enough to Seattle that it was just half a day's drive if she had a yearning to be in a city again. When she first got in Packwood, she was afraid that she might give in and move back east. However, she stuck it out and ended up starting her own business!

Her first night in town, as Lori sat eating dinner at her hotel restaurant, she noticed a sign on a home across her hotel: Business for Sale. While she finished her delicious meal of fresh Alaskan halibut, she asked the server what she knew about the store across the street.

"Actually, you should go over and speak with them. They are moving back east, I think," stated the waitress, whom she came to know as Kim. Kim continued to make small conversation with Lori—not only because she was working for the tip. She was an outgoing young lady—which is important when being a server.

Kim assured Lori that if she went over to talk to them, they would probably give a tour of their home. They lived just above their shop. "They are pretty friendly and won't brush an honest inquiry," she went on to say.

Actually, she did not go and converse with them right away. As Lori lay awake that night on her hotel bed, she wondered if she could be happy here. She tossed and turned half the night, running through her mind different scenarios, but in the end, Lori decided anything would be better than what she left behind. She decided to leave the East Coast after her parents' death, and then finding her boyfriend with someone else was too devastating. Lori made up her mind to talk with the store owners tomorrow.

After waking up early despite her lack of sleep—as she always did even without an alarm clock—Lori went across the street and spoke with the current owners. They introduced themselves as Mr. and Mrs. Stony, and they were selling the business they built and opened twenty years ago.

"We would love to move closer to our grandchildren," they exclaimed almost in unison and said they were selling their store to move to Michigan. The store they owned was on the first floor of a beautiful two-story home located on the main strip in downtown Packwood.

"Please come in," Mrs. Stony said. "I will make some tea."

"Really, I just wanted to know when it would be available," Lori claimed.

Eventually, she did have tea with the Stonys and found that this would be exactly what she was looking for and told them that it was a huge endeavor for her and she would be in contact if she wanted to pursue purchasing their shop and home.

As she was eating her lunch the next day at the hotel restaurant and drinking her daily cup of Earl Grey tea flavored with honey, she watched the building next door. *It is in a good location and is an established business,* she argued silently to herself. Lori already knew that she would not be moving back east and needed somewhere to settle down. This would be perfect; it would become her home *and* her own business! She made up her mind to buy it that day.

Once Lori made her decision, everything seemed to fall into place. Lori was a well-organized person and loved a challenge; therefore, it was easy for her to accomplish everything legally to make the little store in Packwood hers within a very short period.

She met with the Stonys' real estate agent, and once they could agree on a price, the paperwork began. The real estate agent was efficient and made things go smoothly, and by the end of her third week in Washington, Lori had her own business, not to mention her very own place to live. It took them several weeks to get all the legal paperwork together, but the outcome was fruitful.

She had saved the money from the sale of her parents' home back east to fund it, was able to make her changes in both the shop and her new home, and still had a little left over to help her get a good start.

With some work and her personal touches to the store, she reopened it in her own name after a busy two months of planning, painting, and moving. Finding that it would not only be beneficial to her business but would allow her to meet some of the locals, Lori hired many of the workers locally. Only a few repairs to her new shop were called for to make it operable since the owners had kept it up so well.

Lori put in several new shelves that went from floor to ceiling to stock some of the toys she wanted to carry at the front of the store. Her highlights were the traditional toys that were always favorites with most children. Naturally, she decided not to carry some of the new electronic gadgets that were in demand. Lori wanted to be current; however, she knew that it would spread her too thin because these gadgets were always being improved and would have to be updated more frequently than what she had in plan. That type of item would just have to be purchased elsewhere! She wanted to keep her shop, well, pleasant and not complicate things with electronics.

She also had a long table against the length of the back wall for more displays along with some showcases that she acquired from a store in Seattle that was going out of business. Lori's intentions for the showcases were for her to carry some sought-after high-end costume jewelry for the elder women of Packwood.

Lori wanted to carry a little of everything—jewelry, toys, personal items like gloves and some hats, coasters, items with the school's colors that would be a hit with the teens—and was modeling it after some of the novelty shops she knew and loved from Virginia.

There was a back office set up already off to the side and in the back along the stairway to her home. She had replaced the old desk with one that she purchased in Seattle and found a file cabinet that was incredibly functional but classy looking for her record keeping. Besides some good cleaning and a few plants, the only thing she was missing to make it complete was a bowl for Wilhelmina's water.

As far as her living space, Lori replaced the carpet upstairs and taken the wallpaper down from the bathroom. She chose a maroon carpet that would go wonderfully with the wood flooring that just needed a couple of slats replaced. After painting the bathroom a cool ocean green, she was just about set. All she needed to do was get it furnished and decorated—of course not to mention supplying her downstairs store. That would be the fun part!

Buying and decorating her place was very enjoyable; finding the furnishings was exciting as well as therapeutic. Lori was glad she did not marry Michael as they had planned. She and her boyfriend lived together, and everything had to be just so for him, so he chose most of their furniture and about all the decorations. Lori knew that she would not miss the hideous monkey statue he had just at their entryway to their home. She was about as far—physically and emotionally—away now as she could get and loved it. To prove it to herself, she bought a beautiful floral-print sofa that she fell in love with and knew he would have never allowed in their apartment, not to mention that the maroon flecks blended well with the carpet. He would have said it was too loud! She and Michael had completely different decorating ideas, and she was glad that she could finally make her own decisions about her decorating. Other than silly comparisons like that, she never gave him much thought.

Setting up the store was easier than she thought it would be. Many of her ideas for what she wanted to stock were available online. Lori went to Seattle also; she liked to see the quality of items she would make available for purchase, meet the wholesalers and let them be aware of what she expected, and make wonderful contacts in person so that when she placed her orders, they would remember her and hopefully treat her orders with expedience and care.

Her store was novel. Lori carried home decorations like wall hangings, unique candleholders, mirrors, and knickknacks. She also had personal accessories, including silk scarves, broaches, classic perfumes, costume jewelry, and toward the front, an assortment of toys that children never tire of—dolls, stuffed animal bears, model cars for boys, and more of the like.

Lori named it Pleasant Finds. What an enjoyable and rewarding find for her to have acquired the store thusly named. Wilhelmina loved being here also. When they were in Virginia, she was on a leash whenever Lori took her out. Now Wil's leash was retired and hung perpetually on a hook at the front porch. Thankfully, her backyard was large enough for her to run about when she was not able to walk her.

It was perfect. Several months after she took possession of Pleasant Finds, she had a small grand opening. The front entrance was lit up with white Christmas lights to give it a festive air. Helium-filled balloons were given to the children who came with their parents, and Lori had the local store cater the special day. There was also a large cake with her business name wonderfully scrolled with icing to welcome customers who came to celebrate the opening of her shop. As in hopes that the customers would return, she had many flyers that had coupons that would not expire until the following month and a fifty-dollar drawing for a future purchase as well that expired in December.

Lori wanted to call someone and brag of her successfully opening Pleasant Finds and felt a little morose that she had no family to call. She did, however, call her former employer to tell them of her success. They were happy for her and congratulated her for her new beginning.

"Mary! This is Lori. I have some exciting news to share with you!" Lori began. "Remember when I said that I would open my own shop?"

"My word," Mary replied, "I am so proud of you! You will have to send me your new business address so that I can send you some flowers."

"I know that that is something that you have always wanted to do and that if your parents were alive, they would be proud as well," Mary continued. She also went on to say that if Lori needed any help or just support, she should call.

Mary had known Lori for several years and was there for her when her parents had their accident. "Congratulations," she said again after getting Lori's business address and telling her to keep in touch.

Many other shops located on the same street were happy to have her join their community. There was one woman who was a few years older than Lori that especially warmed to her. Her name was Di; she owned the ice cream shop across from her store and was next to the hotel she stayed at when she first moved to Packwood.

"I am so glad that you chose to move here," Di said to Lori. "I have been wondering who would purchase the Stony place! They were so kind, but it is comforting to have someone close to my age that I can connect to," Di exclaimed. They sat up and talked for hours after everyone else left. Di told her that she was a widow who had moved here to Packwood about twelve years ago with her husband. When her husband passed away, she continued to run the ice cream shop. This was her home now.

Lori told her of her exboyfriend in Virginia. Both of her parents had passed on, so when she broke up with Michael, it was a relief to move out here. She actually knew she wanted to move from the East Coast but did not know exactly where.

"I remember a friend of my mother's speaking fondly of Packwood." Lori said, laughingly, that if she did not like it, she would have lived in Seattle. Of course, that would never happen now.

Di and Lori had some tea and exchanged numbers with each other.

"Like you, Earl Grey tea is my favorite too, but I never use honey to sweeten it. This is good!" Di said. She also shared with Lori her favorite grocery shops locally and in Seattle. "When you live in a small community like Packwood," Di told her, "you will want to get bulk items as much as possible when in Seattle." She remembered it as to when she and her late husband lived in the remote bush of Alaska and did their bulk shopping in Anchorage whenever they got a chance to go there. Purchasing items such as nonperishables or paper products online or in bulk when they were in the city sure made a difference in their extra funds.

With the exception of an occasional visit with Di, Lori never got out in the community much. For the most part, when Lori began her new adventure as a new shop owner, she pretty much kept to herself. A lot of her days and evenings were dedicated to making sure her orders were taken care of—ordering, inventorying, delivering on time—and that she was able to price and place them in her shop. This was work but fun work for her.

Of course, she was kind and always courteous to others but never had anyone over for company. A couple of times, Di tried to set her up with someone she knew. Lori would have none of it. Between setting up the store and decorating her home with all her own decorating ideas, she had little time left to do much else.

Lori did however enjoy going to the latest movies and occasionally would invite Di to attend the theater with her, but usually she would go alone. It was neat for her because she could walk to the movie house if she was not going anywhere after the show. She could not have done that in Virginia!

She did, however, have Di come over for dinner, or they would walk together after they both closed their businesses for the day. They eventually became close friends and helped each other out when one or the other was out of town for shopping. Occasionally, Di would walk with Lori and her dog, Wil, to the river just down from the main road.

Except for parents getting toys for their children for various occasions, many of her patrons were from out of town. Many people visited Packwood during the summer or for the holidays; they trekked to or through Packwood, hoping to find novelties, special gift items, or just to get away from the city. Therefore, even though Lori had a little store, she had to keep it fresh and up-to-date with the desires of her customers.

A couple of times a year, Lori would go to Seattle for a buying trip or if she was aching to see a movie that wouldn't be billed at their small theater or to go see a play. This time was special to her. When she lived in Virginia, she would travel to Hampton or even to Williamsburg to see plays occasionally. Lori missed that most of all about living in Virginia. When she found out that the play *Mamma Mia* was showing in Seattle for the next week, she scheduled her buying trip around it. On her last night there, she would see the play. It was showing in April.

When April arrived, Lori went to get new merchandise for her store and attended her play. She did not want her dog confined in a hotel while she was out, so Wilhelmina would stay with Di when she went to town.

"Thank you for watching Wil for me, Di," Lori said. "Is there anything that you would like me to get you while I am in the big city?"

"Listen, Lori, I just had spent some time there last week, and I really don't need anything. You just have a good time," Di told her. "Wil and I will be fine. Don't you worry about us."

Lori brought over Wilhelmina and her food the night before so she could get an early start.

It was a gorgeous day for her drive, and she was thankful that it was not raining when she approached Seattle. There was not much traffic, but she did not take her time and only stopped in Morton to fill her gas tank.

Directly after reaching Seattle, Lori intended on eating lunch at a little place she ate the last time she was there. The name of the restaurant was Gino's. Gino's restaurant was located near the city hall and had a comfortable atmosphere where she could observe the people and watch traffic pass while she ate before she started her shopping. Usually when she was there for lunch, she had a small calzone and a glass of iced tea; however, this time she had a full meal of fresh-cut steak with mashed potatoes and a crisp salad with her iced tea. She felt she would need her energy today.

That was when she met Bill. He was about the same height as her, five feet and eight inches tall, but he had a giant personality. He made her giggle when he first met her. She was just leaving after lunch and was digging in her purse for her keys when he winked at her and stated that if she couldn't find enough change at the bottom of her purse, he was sure they would let her do the dishes!

He introduced himself as Bill Crane. While the waiter was taking her payment, Bill asked if she was from Seattle. Lori said that she was not from there, and they spoke a bit more as they headed out the door. Bill thought Lori was pretty, and suddenly, he asked if she would like to walk a bit with him so they could continue to talk.

Lori did not make a habit of talking to strangers, much less spending the day with someone she just met. However, his smile seemed genuine, and they were in downtown Seattle and surrounded by people. So she relented, deciding that it would be safe to walk a bit with him. They found that they enjoyed talking with each other and ended up walking the whole afternoon.

When it was getting close to dinner, they stopped in a trendy place called Robins' and had a hot sandwich and some sodas for dinner. Bill asked if she was dating or married; she replied no and asked if he was. He had been married, he said, but his wife had passed away a couple of years ago. Lori was watching him when he spoke of his wife and saw that he did love her and he missed her.

Following his wife's passing, he worked at his brother-in-law's lumberyard. He was a high school band teacher but had taken time away from teaching.

He took orders over the phone and kept his entire brother-in-law's employees straight—all eight of them. It was a growing business, so occasionally he had to do hands-on work. He learned how to drive a forklift and did not mind at all when he had to get right into the loading of a customer's order. The physical exertion was healthy for him, but he wanted to begin teaching again.

Their conversation was easy actually; they just were content in their little time together. She was twenty-nine and found out that he was twenty-nine also. He had a sister, and she had no one but her dog, Wil. He went to college, and she chose to jump right into business after having years of working experience for other shops back east.

Bill walked her to her car after they ate.

"I really am glad that you decided to walk with me, Lori!" Bill said, then he shook her hand and gave her a brief hug as a good-bye. Lori drove back to her hotel and wished that she had gotten his number or at least exchanged e-mail addresses. They both relished each other's company, and to the passersby, they could have been a couple. Oh well, she had some shopping to do tomorrow, and the next few days would be busy before she had to head back to Packwood. She did not have time to vie for a man! After her experience with Michael, she was sure she would never be interested in a man again for quite some time. Moreover, her business took up most of her time. That and her trusty dog, Wil, but Wilhelmina did not talk to her late at night when she wanted to rerun her day. Just as well, Wil could not talk back to her!

The last night before heading home, she went to see the play *Mamma Mia*. It was fabulous. As Lori watched it, she could feel the energy and could see the passion in the dancers as they performed. Attending the performance was rejuvenating, and she felt propelled into her new life with song and dance. She was happy about opening her shop and her new life in Packwood, so just being there in the audience made Lori aware of how good things turned out for her so far.

During the intermission, she walked to the concession stand to get a flute of champagne to complete her wonderful evening. It was crowded, and when she turned around, she literally bumped into Bill. When he looked up, he saw Lori in a beautiful flowing black dress that did justice to her curves. Smiling with a smile that reached her heart, he said, "Well, hello there, Lori. How are you?"

When Lori spotted him, she was glad that she had spent the day by getting her haircut along with her manicure. There was a lot of excitement of how the play was going, so she had to lean into him to hear him while he spoke. "Hello to you!" she answered.

"Are you here alone?" he asked. Lori replied yes and that she was glad to bump into him because after their short time together, she wished that she could have gotten his cell number. He was happy to oblige, and they talked about the play, which they both seemed to be enjoying.

It was a short twenty-minute intermission, but he had asked if she would join his table. Then he pointed her toward one of the tables along the wall where there was a lovely woman who was laughing with someone at a nearby table. Alarms went off, and Lori was about to excuse herself when he introduced her to his sister, Jamie.

She was slightly taller than he was, but Lori could see the family resemblance. She wore her hair in a stylish short bob. It fit her face fine.

10

Everything about her was elegant. Lori ran her hand though her hair self-consciously. Jamie put her at ease by extending her hand and saying it was a pleasure to meet her. Bill explained that his sister's husband was not able to attend the play with Jamie, and since she already had two tickets, he came with her. Jamie sort of made him come with her, and now he was glad he did—or he would not have been able to see Lori again!

Jamie was as friendly as her brother Bill was and asked, "Have you eaten yet?" Jamie wanted to invite Lori to have a late dinner after the show. Her husband would be able to join them, and she thought the company would be great.

Lori explained that she had already eaten and that she would be getting up early to drive home tomorrow. Jamie asked her where her home was, and she told her that she lived in Packwood. Jamie explained that they lived in Yakima, not far away from Packwood. Because the play would not end until about ten thirty and it would be too late to drive home, they had a room at the Holiday Inn in downtown Seattle. She also said that she had been to Packwood before for the annual spring festival.

After conversing during the intermission, Jamie could see that the two really complimented each other and wished that they had more time to talk. Jamie thought she and her husband, Don, would have to get Bill along with them to Packwood the next time they went there to visit his family. The house lights blinked, and it was announced that the show was about to begin again. Jamie said good-bye before heading back to her and Bill's seats.

"It was nice to meet you, Jamie," Lori said.

Jamie did not get a chance to tell Lori that her husband was from Packwood and that they went there at least twice a year!

ori went home to Packwood the next morning. It was not too far a drive from Seattle to Packwood. Really, she could make it in half a day's ride, but whenever she went to Seattle, she planned to stay a couple of days and not rush back. Of course, she missed her dog, Wil, but loved to get to the city occasionally. After picking up Wilhelmina, they went home. She put her purchases in the back room to put away later. Then she caught up with her mail before she and Wil went for a walk.

Lori brought a ball to toss for Wil to chase after. She loved being back with her dog. Bending down to Wil, she affectionately rubbed her nose. Lori spoke of her having met Bill. She was talking about him to her dog—now that was silly! Before heading back to Pleasant Finds, Lori stopped at the ice cream shop of Di's so she could thank her for watching her dog and they could chat. Di asked if she had a good trip and if she enjoyed the show.

"It was wonderful!" Lori said with a smile. She always had a delightful smile, but Di could tell that she was not telling her something. Finally, she got Lori to tell her about Bill and Jamie.

Lori was excited and said that while she was at the play, she met the most delightful people; she neglected to tell Di that she and Bill had a wonderful afternoon of walking in Seattle before the play.

They ate dinner together that night at Lori's house. She made them some spaghetti. While she tended to the sauce, Di put together a salad for them. Lori finally told her friend Di the whole story.

She said there was really nothing to tell. Di asked her if she had gotten a number for Bill. She answered, "Yes, but if I didn't run into Bill at the play, I considered looking his brother-in-law's business number up and calling him instead."

Now that was a huge clue, thought Di. She could tell that Lori liked him and continued to ask about her evening at the play. She was glad to see her new friend excited about someone. When she asked Lori if they planned to see each other again soon, Lori said, "I really don't want to start anything. Besides, I just met the man, and he lives half a day's ride away from here!"

Because it was almost time for the spring festival, all the shops were jazzing up their storefronts. Lori was also. Her theme, as well as most of the shops, was celebrating spring with large displays of flowers and colors.

She ordered two large arrangements of flowers for the storefront and a dozen roses for her counter. Setting up her store for this special occasion was fun. So many times when she was a child and shopping with her mother, Lori wished that she could own a store. Never in her wildest dreams did she think it would happen. It was possible, however, because when her parents passed on, they left their home to her, and she sold it when she moved to Packwood. That gave her funds to acquire Pleasant Finds.

Many of the businesses joined in and decorated Main Street. Lori volunteered and got to know a few more people of her new city. They put up some flags along the electrical poles and hung a banner at the main entrance to Packwood. There were vendors set up outside to sell their crafts along the shops, and many restaurants put shaded umbrella tables out and cooked on large grills outside for this occasion. There was even a local man who hired his ponies for pony rides for the children and several bands that would take turns on playing on a stage, including the high school's band to march in the parade.

The official day of the festival was the last Saturday of May, but the excitement lasted throughout the week. The hotels were booked, and there were plenty of people spending their money at all the shops and restaurants. There were many new faces about town, and there was an expectant air about town because all the events led to Saturday. On Saturday, there would be a parade and then a dance in the evening at the town hall.

I t was Thursday, and she had just closed the shop for the day. Someone knocking excitedly on her front door while she was heading upstairs to her apartment to get Wil's ball startled Lori. She was going to change into some jeans before taking Wil out. As she descended the stairway, she turned around and saw through the window a boy and a couple of girls that she had seen in her shop before.

When Lori opened the door, the young man stated that he was selling space in the high school yearbook and wanted to know if she would be a sponsor. Two giggling teenage girls accompanied him. They were selling advertising space to sponsors and wanted to know if she wanted to support them by buying space for her business name in the yearbook.

"There are lots of businesses who are placing a sponsor page for advertising," he voiced with a confident sales pitch.

"Actually, that would be a good idea," Lori returned.

The young boy introduced himself as Jerry, and his friends were a couple of cheerleaders—Sue and Kim—he knew from school.

"Please come in. Who do I make the check out to?" inquired Lori. Lori invited them into her store while she wrote a check. She asked them if they were going to be in the parade on Saturday.

"We will!" the girls chimed in cadence, right on cue like any cheerleader would, and then giggled again.

Jerry, however, said that he would not be in the parade and went on to say that he would be out drumming up as many sponsors as he could that weekend.

He told Lori that he also took photographs for the yearbook.

"You are the school photographer?" She said that was wonderful.

She thought that this was a profitable idea and was a low cost for advertising and asked him how much extra it would be if her storefront could be included.

Jerry told her that he thought it would be twenty-five dollars more. "I will be back in touch with you by Saturday."

The girls looked around the shop while Jerry was speaking with Lori and then asked if it was too late to buy some hair accessories to match their cheerleading outfits.

"No, and please tell the rest of your cheerleading squad to come in, and I will give you a 5 percent discount," Lori replied.

After the girls made their purchase, Jerry thanked her again and said he would try to get back with her before Saturday.

"Thanks," the girls were yelling as they left. Just then, the phone rang.

Wil was practically under her feet when she reached for the phone. Wilhelmina wanted to go for their walk and wanted to go now. The voice on the other side sounded familiar as she noted on her caller ID that it was from the Lodge. She realized after a moment that it was Jamie. It was Bill's sister. She and Don, her husband, had just arrived with Bill from Yakima and were staying at the Lodge.

"We were wondering if you would like to eat dinner with us?" said Jamie from the other end of the line. *This is fabulous*, thought Lori.

Wow! Well, she did have to eat, and she thought it would be nice to see Bill again.

"I just have to take my dog for a short walk first, and then I will be glad to meet you all." Lori let Jamie know that she would be taking her dog out for a walk and then she could meet them at the Lodge in about an hour.

Jamie said that would be fine and hung up. Lori replaced the phone, ruffled Wil's head, and kissed her. "Let's go!" she called to Wil.

Lori practically floated as she was walking Wil; she was hoping to call Bill and could not even begin to know how to prelude her call! Wil, who was naturally excited to go for a walk, really enjoyed her enthusiasm although Wil thought it was just to be out with her again! They walked around their route twice that day in all the excitement.

When she was done walking Wil, she led her home and put her in the house before heading out to meet up at the Lodge with Jamie, her husband, and Bill. With all this excitement, she never did get to change to her jeans, and she was glad that she did not because Lori noticed that the Lodge was not about fancy sit-down dinners.

She walked directly to the restroom to let her hair down from a bun and got a quick look at herself before she met Bill again. Pleased with her reflection, she took a deep breath and went to meet her party.

When she walked into the dining room, she did not have a hard time finding them. The dinner crowd had pretty much left, and they were watching for her. Bill stood up and waved her to their table.

"Hello," he said as he gave her a hug. Smiling, he said that he was very happy to see her again.

"Ahem," Jamie cleared her throat, and Bill realized that he had not introduced Don. Don, Jamie's husband, was easygoing and got everyone laughing with his easygoing personality.

"I'm Don," Jamie's husband said, "her better half."

Jamie said that they just arrived that afternoon and were staying until Sunday.

Lori found out during their conversation at dinner that Bill would be staying a bit longer. He had an interview at the high school. Lori could tell that Jamie was pleased with his decision to move on with his career. Jamie was just pleased because it meant that possibly Bill and Lori would be able to spend more time together.

"Bill might be taking a teaching position at Packwood High," Jamie explained. His interview was scheduled for the upcoming Monday.

She found out that she really knew little of him and was glad that she had the opportunity to find out more about Bill. Seeing him in the company of his sister and brother-in-law made him relaxed, and the conversation was light. He taught band, and there was going to be an opening at the Packwood High that fall.

My god, her head was spinning! *We may see more of each other!* she thought. She now regretted that she did not know more people in Packwood and made a mental note to get out and meet more people. Right now, she was wishing she knew someone other than Jerry and his two friends from the high school.

Jamie said that it was about time that Bill moved out of his house in Yakima—it was nothing but memories of his wife. She did not mean it wickedly; Jamie just did not want him sitting around alone any longer. Two years of grieving was enough!

Don agreed but moved the conversation to Lori's shop and asked how business was doing.

"How do you like our little town?" Don asked after asking how her sales were. He was just trying to get Jamie and Bill off the conversation of his wife.

Bill got along well with his sister and her husband, and it was a wonderful evening. They all ordered, and Don said that he would like to pick up the check and that he did not want this to be their last encounter.

While they waited for their food to arrive, they spoke a bit more, and it seemed to be as if they were friends for a long time.

When they were finished with their meal, they went to the lounge, listened to music, and continued to talk. Bill even asked Lori to dance. She had not danced since high school, but he promised her that he would not step on her toes. His sister and Don danced also, then Don cut in, and while they were dancing, Lori was surprised to learn that Don was from Packwood. He moved to Yakima when he met Jamie. That was where she and Bill lived most of their life. When they were young, their family moved there from Seattle to get away from the city.

Jamie was getting tired and bid her brother and Lori good night. "Will you take an old gal home?" she asked Don. Don slipped his arm around her as if she was an invalid and said, jokingly, "Why certainly, deary, wouldn't want you to expire here."

Don said they enjoyed meeting Lori, and they all agreed that they would see each other the next day for sure. Bill drove her home since she walked there, and it had started to rain.

When they got to her storefront, she asked him if he wanted to come up for some coffee.

"I can make some coffee if you would like," she said lightly. He said that would be nice, and they climbed up to her house above the store.

There were stairs that led to the top of her living quarters at the back of the store, and after closing the door, she led the way up to her home. Wil greeted them; she was happy to see her master and was curious of their company. Bill asked how long she had lived here, and she told him that it was just over a year and a half now.

They sat at her kitchen table while the coffee was brewing. He commented how quaint her place looked and stated that it was nicely decorated. She was beaming; he was her first guest other than Di up to her place. Actually, since her breakup with Michael, this was the first time she spent any time with another man, so she felt nervous, but Bill was kind and fun. By the time they had their first cup of coffee, she was relaxed.

After he had coffee with her and they had a chance to get to know each other a bit more, Bill noticed that it was getting late. "I best get going," Bill said.

As Lori walked him down, he reached for her hand. Bringing it to his face, he told her that he had a wonderful time and would bring his sister and Don tomorrow to see her shop. Just before he left, he leaned forward and gently touched her cheek with his lips.

"Good night, young lady," he said.

Grieved, Lori watched him leave and thought she would never get to sleep! She could feel the heat that he stirred in her.

Eventually, sleep did come but not without dreamy thoughts of Bill and the fact that there might be something starting here, and she was elated and scared at the same time. Before she fell asleep, Lori held hope for a relationship to build between them.

The next morning, shortly after hanging out her Open sign, customers came and left, making her morning go fast. She was watching for Bill and his family to come. Just after lunch, they did arrive, and Jamie adored the shop.

"Hello," she called out as they walked through the door. Lori was hoping to get a chance to chat again but knew that it would be a busy day for her. Jamie found a couple of items she purchased to give as gifts and bought a silk scarf for herself. Bill and Don waited patiently for her. They lightheartedly teased her, saying that Jamie could not pass up any store, but they were not upset that she took her time. It was evident that they were a loving group who liked to joke with each other.

Lori said that there would be a parade tomorrow, and that if they would like to, they could watch from her storefront porch.

"That would be great!" They all agreed, but they warned her that some of Don's family would be with them. Lori said that it would not be a problem. They planned to be there around nine thirty.

Jamie and Don went out to look at the happenings; Bill stayed and talked with Lori a while longer, and when customers came, he observed her and liked what he saw. She was a pretty woman with a kindness about her with her customers. She was definitely a likable person.

Six o'clock came fast; she sold a bunch of items and had sold quite a lot of high-ticket items too. Bill asked her if she had any plans; he did not want to leave her company.

Lori said "Wil and I will be going for a walk" and invited Bill to come along. Wil stayed with Lori in the shop and did not mind any customers, but when it was closing time, she wanted that walk!

Whenever Lori mentioned *walk* to Wilhelmina, she would bound out the door. Her steps were a little jauntier, and she chased about in circles until they crossed the front door. There was a lot of traffic because of the festivities, but most of it was pedestrian right now, so Lori was not too worried about Wil.

They started to walk toward the river, and Bill took her hand. "I am glad to see you," he stated. It felt good. Lori looked at him to check him out as he was talking to her. She liked everything that she had seen so far, and they continued toward the river.

He was asking her a question, and she had to ask him to repeat the question because her mind was elsewhere. He had light-blue eyes that contrasted with his dark hair that was intriguing. He asked her again if she had seen any elk during the winter around the river when she was walking.

"I have," Lori told him. She also told Bill that sometimes she was worried "that Wil would try to chase them. Thankfully up to now, the elk and Wil don't seem the least bit bothered by the other."

"Are you excited about the possibility of being hired on and living in Packwood?" Lori asked. Bill told her he would like it very much to get back into teaching—that was his first love. However, he was also happy that it would give him a chance to get to know her better.

They followed Wil around the bank of the river, and then they walked back toward her store. It was a nice spring evening, and it was warm enough that they did not need any jackets even that late in the evening.

God, it was good that winter was almost over; although, compared to many places, it was not as harsh as winter could be. There were new blossoms and birds flitting about, and everything was greener now that the days were warmer and longer.

When they neared her store, Lori let Wil into the backyard, and then she invited Bill to eat with her. She said there was a great Chinese food takeout that would deliver, and while they were waiting for it, they could get to know each other better.

She pulled out a flyer with a menu on it, and after they decided on what they both would like to eat, Lori placed the order.

"Hello, I would like to place a delivery order, please," she began when the man at the other end of the phone answered. After telling the restaurant where to make the delivery, the voice at the other end of the phone said that it would take about thirty minutes.

Before dinner arrived, she changed into some sweatpants to be comfortable. Bill called his sister and Don to let them know that he was with Lori. Lori turned on some music, and they both sat on the sofa and suddenly got quiet.

"Hey!" she said. "What do you think of Packwood?" That was when Bill replied that if all the people were as nice as she was, then he would love to teach here. Then he confessed that he had been here many times with his sister and her husband Don.

He further went on to say that Don's family lived here. Her face blushed because she was intently watching his eyes as he spoke. She was thankful that the delivery person rang her bell just then.

Bill went to the door and paid for the order. Wilhelmina, smelling the food, came in when Bill was getting the food. Lori got some wine and set some plates for them on the table. It was take-out food, but she served it on her dinner plates as proud as if she cooked it herself.

"Have you used chopsticks before?" Lori asked. Bill laughed and said, "If I use them, Wil will be getting more of the food than I will!"

Wil lay quietly under the table, waiting for them to finish so she could get any leftovers or food that may have found its way to the floor.

While they were eating and enjoying each other's company, they stopped and gazed into each other's eyes and realized that they had yearnings for each other. Lori did not want him to be just a fling though and was worried that he may not take the position at the school and they would never see each other again.

Still they kissed despite all her misgivings. The feeling was sensational—mostly because neither one of them had been intimate with anyone else in quite some time. He leaned across the table and moved his hand to cup her face, and she eased her hand behind his neck to pull him closer.

"Lori," Bill said, "I think I am falling in love." Lori's heart beat faster, and she felt a twinge in her stomach, longing for this to last.

Their kiss was full of desire. They probably would have gone straight to the couch or the floor if the phone had not interrupted them. It was a wrong number.

That was just the cue needed to cool things off! Lori shook her head and let out a sigh. Bill chuckled and ran his hand through his hair. "I better get going," he said. Yep, that was close.

He let himself out, and then Lori sat on her couch and damned the phone. She did have a busy day tomorrow though and needed to get some sleep. As she showered, she wondered how it would feel if she had Bill to wash her back. Good grief! Getting goofy ideas and ahead of herself, huh? All they did was kiss. It was a while before she fell asleep.

The next morning—when she saw Jamie, Don, Bill, and several members of Don's family arrive—she recognized two of the women as patrons to her shop. It was nice to meet them officially, and they were as happy as Jamie was that Bill had finally met someone.

Lori was worried that perhaps Jamie could sense they had kissed; if she had noticed, she never let on. Bill did lean in and peck her cheek when he saw her and said his hello as if he had known her forever. Such a comfortable and filling feeling it was to have attention from him.

The parade was short, but everyone had fun. Lori had seen the two cheerleaders that stopped by with Jerry from the school yearbook. They waved to her, and she had told Bill, "There are the two girls I told you about. They look cute in their uniforms."

Bill told her that one of them was a niece of Don's. "Sue," he called out. "Hello!" Bill walked up to the band director when it was over and greeted her. She was glad to see him; they had met before through Don and his family.

Jan, the band director, told him that this was her last event with the group before she moved on. Her husband was being transferred to Oregon. This would be a great move for them because they would be closer to his family. The director was hoping that he would take the position and told him that the children here were lovely to work with.

Lori returned to her shop and was followed by Jamie. Bill and Don were going fishing with some of their friends and family.

"See you later, Jamie!" Don called to his wife. She waved to him and her brother. Jamie smiled and asked if Lori liked Bill. Of course, she knew the answer, but she wanted to hear Lori say so. After they visited for a short while, customers started coming in. Jamie was leaving, but before she left, she asked Lori to join them again for dinner.

Before Lori closed her shop, Jerry stopped by her store to let her know that if she wanted to have a picture of the store in their yearbook, it would be just the twenty-five dollars as he said. She agreed to do this and wrote him another check.

"Are you from Packwood?" she asked.

He was of course; actually, he was born here, he said.

"Well, it was nice to talk to you." Then Jerry asked if he could stop by again to say hello when he got a chance. This made her happy. Lori realized that Di would be proud of her too. She was getting to know a few more people from her new hometown.

Bill picked her up in his car that night. Everyone would be going to the dance at the town hall after dinner, and he would be driving. He also thought it would be a chance to take Lori for a drive.

A band from Yakima played, and everyone was enjoying the music. Bill and Lori danced practically every dance.

As they were dancing, Bill asked Lori if she was having a good time. "Of course, I have a great partner to dance with," she said.

Don and Jamie had fun too, but they were getting tired and reminded Bill that he said he would take them back to the Lodge.

"When I am done driving you two back to the Lodge," he told them, "I will be going to take Lori around and show her where Don's family lives." He continued to say that he would not be out too late, and they answered, "Take your time, Bill."

Lori rode with Bill when he drove them back to the Lodge. After they walked Don and Jamie to the entrance from the parking lot and said good night, they strolled around the grounds at the Lodge.

The grounds had some very nice sculptured hedges and a path that wound around the back toward the mountains and ended at a bench surrounded by some fragrant spring flowers. There was a bench in a secluded spot, and they stopped for a moment and talked awhile.

"I really like your family, Bill," Lori said. As she was talking, he moved his hand from hers and laid it against her shoulder. "They like you too," he answered.

Then they behaved like two teenagers in lust and began kissing as soon as they were out of everyone's sight. Neither of the two of them noticed that it had gotten a little cooler that night.

This time, it was sweet, and he held her closely for a moment. It seemed like an eternity before they walked back to his car, but it had not been that long really. He asked if she really wanted to see where Don's family lived.

"On the other hand," he stated, "would you rather go somewhere else?" Lori sensed that they could use some private time together and invited him to her place. They drove to her home and practically raced up the stairs to her home. As always, Wil greeted her. However, tonight, all Lori could do was give Wilhelmina a pat on the head. Wil gave a little whimper and lay down on her bed by the door.

By the time they reached the top of the steps, they were groping at each other, embraced in hungry kisses. She paused long enough to open the door, and once they were in, they continued to kiss, and Bill pushed the door shut with his foot.

They moved to the couch, and Bill was practically on top of her. The room was heating up; he held her close, and neither one of them could possibly stop. Every moment seemed to take forever but not quite long enough. Once they were sated, they could look at this situation and decide if they both wanted something more than just a brief encounter. He wanted to tell her he loved her. She had no idea how, but Lori wanted this to last forever.

They got up and ate a snack of cheese and crackers along with a glass of wine despite the dinner they ate not long ago. Everything started all over again after they had energized themselves. First, it was just a touch, and then it exploded beyond feeling. Their hungry bodies never quite got enough of each other.

Bill ended up staying the night, and before he left that morning to see his sister and brother-in-law off, they made love again. Their bodies were hurting for each other, and they could not seem to get enough of each other.

In the morning, Bill realized that he would have to get the teaching position here in Packwood! Just leaving her when he left to say good-bye to his sister and her husband was taking him away from his newfound lover.

"If you would like to wait until after I say good-bye to my sister and Don, I will take you to eat something," Bill said. It really did not matter to either of them where they went to eat; just that they would get to spend more time together would be fine.

"Sure, Bill, just return when you are finished," Lori said. "I will be waiting. Maybe we could walk Wil together too." She had not had a chance to let her out yet.

Once Jamie and Don left, Bill took Lori out to eat brunch. They were both hungry. It was Sunday, and the town was quiet after the festival. They were both as happy as they could be, just sitting across from each other. The waitress, who had seen Lori about town and had actually been to her shop a couple of times, stated to Lori that it was good to see her.

"Do you know the waitress?" asked Bill. No, Lori exclaimed, but she answered, "She was probably wondering if I was a nun or something!"

Lori said that this was the first time that the people of Packwood had seen her with someone other than Di or her dog, Wil.

Bill said, "I am hoping that will change soon."

Bill wanted to spend the rest of his days with this delightful woman named Lori who owned Pleasant Finds.

They finished their brunch, tipped the waitress, and left hand in hand.

The two left the restaurant and went straight to her house. "We still have to take Wilhelmina for a walk," Lori said, smiling.

Bill spent the day with her and Wil. They went for a walk to the school to get a glance at where he might work.

He wanted to stay the night when Lori asked him to stay, but he frowned because he knew he had his interview the next day.

"If I stay," he said, "we will not get much rest."

So after they ate dinner at her house and he helped Lori with her dishes, Bill returned to the Lodge. Lori locked the door after he left, and she plopped on her bed with her hands spread out above her head and laughed.

"What a wonderful few days I have had!" she exclaimed out loud to no one. But she had to state it; it was hard to believe it herself.

First thing Monday morning, she called him before he left for his interview and wished him luck. "I will be thinking positive thoughts for your interview, Bill. Good luck!" she said.

Lori opened her shop and did not think that she would hear from Bill until later that day, but before his interview, he stopped by and gave her some beautiful and fragrant roses that he picked up in the florist shop in the grocery store.

"I just wanted to thank you for everything, and I loved spending the last few days with you." Then he kissed her cheek before he left. Lori waved with a smile of her own and said, "Good luck again."

His interview went swimmingly. After speaking with the secretary, Bill met John, who was the principal for Packwood High.

"My name is John. It is good to meet you," he said. "I've known your brother-in-law for a while now," he said as he gripped his hand for a shake.

"The job is yours if you want it because I know from Don and his family that you are a good man," John said.

"I have also reviewed your résumé and contacted your previous school. They told me great things about you." He was impressed with his résumé, the principal told him. Then John went on to say that the budget would also allow him to take one class for a trip to Seattle for the music festival the next spring.

Bill had hardly a chance to get a word in. Obviously, he would be welcomed here at Packwood High if he would just sign on. From what he could see, he thought he would like the school.

"We would love to have you join our team!" said John. "If you would like to come in this afternoon, I can have my secretary bring you around and meet some of the other faculty."

"Thank you," Bill replied. "I am glad to have this opportunity." Prior to the interview, he wasn't sure if he would take the teaching position, but after he saw the band room and all the other equipment that was available, not to mention all the benefits he was offered, he'd be crazy not to take the job. The staff was very encouraging too and seemed happy for the most part about teaching at Packwood High.

The principal shook his hand when they were through and said, "Very nice to meet you, Bill, and I hope to hear of your decision soon."

"I really would like to accept your offer," Bill told John. However, he needed to make a couple of contact calls. Bill was thinking of his job in Yakima and how much notice he would have to give before he can move.

He was so happy that he was whistling as he left the school. He was walking with a spring in his step as he skipped down the stairway.

Upon reaching his vehicle, he drove directly to Pleasant Finds, and while he was opening the door, he announced to Lori that he would be taking the teaching position by saying, "Guess who will be tooting his own horn soon at Packwood High?" He knew he sounded corny, but nothing could curb his excitement.

Bill's biggest worry was whether his house in Yakima would sell; that was the only thing holding him back. Bill called a real estate broker that evening and put his home on the market.

He would be keeping just a few pieces of his furniture, not wanting too many memories of his deceased wife. That meant he would be having yard sales and making donations on his off time.

On his trips home from work, Bill would pick up boxes and stop by Walmart to get some yard sale signs and any other items that he needed to hurry his move to Packwood.

He listed his items for sale in the *Yakima Trading* paper and posted signs up at different locations, the library, and a couple of stores near his place and at the church. Posting everything that was for sale on Craigslist helped too.

Lena called from his church; she wanted a couch and a kitchen table. All she required was that the table matched the chairs she had already bought elsewhere.

It was not too long before many of his items were gone. He contacted the church Don and Jamie attended and let them announce what he would have for free to give away. First come, first serve. Blankets, some towels that were for the guest room, as well as the bedding from his and his deceased wife's room. He wanted a fresh start and needed no reminders of her.

Cleaning out his place was a double-edged knife; he missed his wife, but it gave him a chance to say good-bye to her again. The best part, he reflected, was that he would be taking up teaching again and would be close to Lori.

He planned to list the house at the appraised price and go down if he needed to lower the price, but he did not have to. He had gotten lucky, and it sold soon—even in this unsound economy. That was where the saying "Location, location, location!" fell true. In addition, it didn't hurt that he had kept his home well maintained.

Until his house in Yakima closed, he would be living there, but in the meantime, he would also be looking for an apartment in Packwood that would be close to the school.

He called the principal directly after that and told him again that he would be taking the teaching position that fall.

"I didn't get the price that I asked for, but the folks who wanted to purchase it made it impossible to say no to their offer—especially in this real estate market," Bill told his sister Jamie when he called to let her know that it sold. It would not be much longer, and he would be moving to Packwood.

Jamie and Don were happy that he would be starting a new life; this was the first move he made away from his life with his deceased wife.

Jamie and Don were happy for him and had a going-away party for him. They invited a small crowd. Besides themselves, there were a couple of the guys from the lumberyard along with their families. They had barbecued steaks with all the fixings. For the kids, they grilled some hot dogs and let them roast marshmallows.

"We are going to miss you, Bill," said several of his coworkers, but they knew that he missed teaching and needed to get on with his life. Most of them knew people in Packwood and traveled there a couple of times a year, so they would always be in contact with him. If not, they could find out how he was doing through Jamie.

Jamie and Don could not stop smiling; they had a good feeling about the move for him. They were as excited as Bill was about his move. They were equally happy that Lori might be a big part of it.

Within three weeks, Bill moved to Packwood and into an apartment not too far from the high school. He spent most of his time between the school and Pleasant Finds. He was taking inventory of the instruments and their conditions. He also was planning his schedule for his upcoming classes. He had a lot to do before school started, but he found time to spend with Lori.

Lori started to meet more people of Packwood since she and Bill were dating. Sometimes after she closed shop, Lori would walk Wil toward the school instead of the river. Wilhelmina did not mind, though, as long as she got out.

On the Fourth of July, Don and Jamie came out to visit and were glad to see that Bill and Lori were getting along. There was a party at the Lodge for the town to celebrate the Fourth, and the city of Packwood put on a wonderful display of fireworks just beyond the river. Some locals had to be reminded to just watch the fireworks and not set off their own because there was a possibility of starting a forest fire. The night was a success though. The police only had to give out a couple of warnings.

Lori introduced Jamie to Di when she stopped by their table to say hello. Di said that she knew Don's family and that they were friends for many years! Lori was seeing what a small world it could be and was once again thankful for her luck.

Jamie and Lori loved to spend time together on her visits. Mostly, it was just fun to have someone new to talk with. They both loved going to Seattle and always talked of their favorite places to visit.

Lori told Jamie that on her next trip, Bill was heading into Seattle with her, and they would be staying together since they would be taking only one car. This made Jamie wonder if this was serious. She was smiling when she asked jokingly if they needed a chaperone.

Time flew by; it was almost the end of August. They would be driving to Seattle in Bill's car. Bill was purchasing furniture for his new apartment, and Lori was getting items for sale in her shop. She wanted him to move in with her, but he did not want to if they were not married.

The last night they were in Seattle, they went to eat at the Space Needle restaurant. It was a spectacular sight. Lori had been to the top of the Needle only as a sightseer and during the day. Being there at night was exciting, and the city looked like a completely different world. It was more exciting because Bill had purchased an engagement ring that afternoon while she was out shopping for her store.

"Will you marry me, Lori?" When Bill asked her to marry him, she could only just nod her head, afraid to speak because she was so happy that she could cry. He had picked a beautifully romantic spot and made her feel very special.

"I love you, Bill" was what Lori was finally able to voice once she gathered herself.

After they got back to their hotel, Bill had to go and tie up his delivery orders with his furniture because they would be returning in the morning. While he was gone, Lori called Jamie; she was too excited to keep this to herself. They were both happy!

Lori had not stopped smiling all evening, and Jamie could hear it in her voice. Before they said good-bye, Jamie told Lori that she was glad that she would be part of their family. Both she and Don believed they made a perfect couple and were hoping for this since they met her.

When they returned to Packwood, school started shortly afterward. Bill was busy and so was Lori. All the kids were coming to her shop to buy back-to-school items that she carried. Her store was becoming a general store as she added the items to pacify her customers.

While they were in Seattle, she was able to pick up a lot of the required back-to-school items to supply her shop. The locals were excited to have a new teacher and to get to know her intended. Lori actually spent more time in the community now and had gotten to know a bit more of her town. She helped with fund-raisers when she had time. It did feel like her town now that Bill was with her.

They got married at the Lodge in September, and he moved in with her. The furniture that he had purchased were items that they picked out together, so she liked them, and they blended well with what she already had. What they could use, they brought to her home. So their living quarters would not be cramped, everything else was given to Don's family or sold in a yard sale.

Di was her matron of honor, and Jamie was in charge of all the doings for the reception. It went without any hitches, and everyone was having a fun time at their reception that took place in her backyard. Lori could not be happier. Wilhelmina liked the new addition to their little home too.

Jamie asked if they were going to take time off for a honeymoon and if they had any idea where they wanted to go. They both had things to do at that time of the year, so they planned to go on a honeymoon sometime further in their marriage. It was not an issue; they were just both glad to be married. Everything seemed to be going well for them.

They did, however, spend two nights, all expenses paid by Don, at the Lodge. "It is the least Jamie and I can stand for. We, after all, went for a month away on our honeymoon to Tahiti."

Jerry, the boy who sold Lori some space in the local yearbook, started coming around a lot after school. Evidently, his parents had gotten divorced recently, and he told Bill and Lori that since his mom worked nights, he had time to visit them.

Lori ended up hiring him to help at the shop. He stocked, ran the register, and helped her overall with keeping the store. He also brought in an untapped market; she did not realize how popular Jerry was despite his home situation. Teenagers were coming in her shop more often than not and not only girls! Many of the young men came to shoot the breeze with him, and this made for great business.

She dedicated a corner of her store to the colors of the high school. Lori also had on display the current yearbook and school events posted behind the "Packwood's High School" table. Her little store was beginning to carry quite a variety along with other school supplies that she began to carry.

They found out that Jerry was in the yearbook club, but as far as any other school involvement went, that was it. He was having a difficult time accepting his parents' divorce; he could not accept the fact that his family was torn apart. At sixteen, it was maddening for him to deal with many things, much less a divorce.

Bill was busy with his classes, trying to get a Christmas concert together and dealing with many practices that went late. He asked Jerry if he wanted to join the band; he said no, but he said he would like to help Bill when they set up for concerts or have fund-raisers.

Jamie and Don were coming for the holidays for a visit, but they would be staying at his family's home. Everyone was excited; they would be eating Christmas dinner with Bill and Lori.

Just before Christmas, Lori found out she was pregnant—actually, about two months pregnant! Both she and Bill were very happy. Life seemed wonderful for them. After her appointment with the doctor, she called him at work to let him know of her pregnancy.

"We have been blessed," Lori said to Bill. That was how she began to explain her doctor's appointment.

"You have made me the happiest man so many times since I have known you, Lori. Thank you. I love you too," Lori heard her husband say.

In addition, Lori could not contain herself; she had yet to tell Jamie and Don that she and Bill were expecting a child!

Lori was giving great sales, and the store was busy this time of the year, so Bill helped her with most of the dinner. They did not actually have to prepare a whole lot for dinner because now that Jamie found out that Lori was pregnant, Jamie said that she would bring a pie and a ham. If they would just have a salad and some potatoes, the meal would be complete.

"Are you sure that won't be a problem for you? You know that I am just pregnant—it's not as if I am helpless!" exclaimed Lori.

"Not at all! I enjoy cooking, and I can't wait to see you and Bill. Don will be glad that I am making myself useful." This was untrue; Don always appreciated Jamie, and everyone could see it.

When Jamie and Don heard of Jerry before dinner as they sat in the living room and caught up on each other's lives, they asked Lori if it was wise to let him come over so often.

"I mean, I don't want his parents to get angry with you two," said Don. This concern was understandable; they all heard about the murders that happened the past fall that a man committed after a long and ugly divorce.

Both Bill and Lori said there was nothing wrong with Jerry coming over; they loved him as a son. Besides, he was great company and a big help to them both.

During their conversations, Don and Jamie learned that Jerry's parents were married until he turned fifteen. They had lived in Packwood all his life, and now his family was split up. He and his mom remained here, but his father had moved to Seattle.

Jerry missed the security he had when his family was together and felt like he was being crushed. His heart raced, and he could hardly breathe most times. Many of his friends at school knew his family and did not speak to him as freely as they had before because the rumor was that his mother was being unfaithful. This burned Jerry, so he just did not stay home as much. Since she and his father got divorced, his mother had been drinking a lot and would not go into work on time on some days.

Jerry confided in Bill about these and other atrocities. They could not turn him away when all Jerry needed was someone to listen to him without feeling judged.

If he were any other kid, he would have started drinking or at least would have run away by now. Thank God, he had not started experimenting with drugs. This was a problem for any normal young man his age. His peers had a big influence on him as it was, but somehow he managed to stay out of that scene. He and his mom yelled at each other on most nights. If his father wanted him to, he would have went to live with him, but his father wanted no reminders of Jerry's mom. It was because of Bill and Lori's encouragement that he stayed straight and continued to go to school.

During Christmas dinner, while Jamie and Lori were setting the table and Bill and Don were watching television, the doorbell chimed. When Bill answered it, he found Jerry skulking against the door and crying.

"My god, Jerry, are you okay?" Bill asked. Jerry asked if he could come in.

"Of course, please," Bill answered. He put his arm around Jerry and led him into the hallway.

They all heard the conversation through the entryway, and Lori suggested that Jamie and Don go with her to see her new Christmas selections that she had for sale. Lori quietly led them down the back stairway to give Bill a chance to talk to Jerry privately.

Bill found out Jerry's mom and her boyfriend were drinking. That was why Jerry did not want to be there.

"Hey, let's go out and see Wil," Bill encouraged. "A bit of fresh air always helps clear the head."

Bill was hoping that seeing Wil would cheer Jerry up. Bill led Jerry out and took him down to the backyard to talk. Jerry said that if his mother kept seeing this man, he would run away! Bill advised him against this and said that they should eat dinner, and then they could figure out what to do.

It was a quiet dinner. Bill introduced Jerry to Jamie and Don. Bill sat opposite from Lori while they ate their meal, and she kept trying to gauge the enormity of the situation with Jerry. Bill just kept smiling and eating; occasionally, he would wink at Jerry.

Lori kept trying to keep the subject light and talked about the Christmas shows that were playing on television. Usually, when Lori and Jamie got together, they were so happy to catch up on each other's lives that Bill and Don could hardly get any words in edgewise.

Jerry ate but not very much. Don and Jamie left after they helped with the dishes. Jamie said that she would call when they got back to Yakima. They went to Don's family's house before leaving in the morning.

"Merry Christmas!" they said to everyone as they left before they hugged Bill and Lori. It did not feel that merry to Jerry though.

ill told Jerry that they should call his mom and let her know where he was. He said that they probably would not even answer the phone, but he did call because Jerry was worried about his mom. He ended up leaving a message with the Cranes' number on their machine. He was right about them not answering. Jerry just hoped that his mom would not drink too much.

In the end, Jerry stayed the night. They had plenty of room, and while Lori made up the extra room for him, Bill tried to relax Jerry by asking him about his Christmas morning. This seemed to put Jerry out more, so they played catch with Wil in the backyard.

That night, as Jerry was sleeping, Lori and Bill discussed what happened that evening. They were worried for him and felt they were fortunate that he came to them. More importantly, they needed to talk to his mom to find out what was going on.

Because of the holidays, the shop would be closed until the twenty-seventh of December. Bill had no school until January 3. They had a few days to decide what they would do about Jerry. Lori and Bill let him sleep in the next morning while Bill went and spoke with the school counselor.

The counselor said that Jerry, who was usually an average student, has been having a bad time at school since his parents divorced. He had been talking to him, but Jerry clammed up whenever the counselor asked him about his family. The counselor stated that Bill knew more than he did. Something would have to work out and soon; this was too destructive to Jerry's life!

When Jerry awoke, he hesitantly walked into the kitchen. Lori greeted him with a good morning and a rub on his shoulders. She asked him what he would like for breakfast. Jerry looked around nervously and said that maybe he needed to get home. He was embarrassed about last night. Lori told him that was silly.

"What we need is a good breakfast. Let's have some eggs and bacon before Bill gets home."

Jerry asked where Bill was; he felt closer to him really. Lori told him that he had errands to run that morning and that he would be back shortly. While she was making the breakfast, Lori asked Jerry if he would let Wil in; she had been let out early that morning when Bill left.

Jerry was glad for the distraction because he felt horrible. Food was not what he was thinking about! After playing with Wilhelmina for a while though, he ate with Lori. His appetite was the only thing normal for this teenager right now.

He ate a plate full of scrambled eggs, five pieces of bacon, and two pieces of toast with jelly. He did not realize just how hungry he was. As they were finishing their breakfast, Bill returned. He went over, kissed Lori, and gave Jerry a squeeze on his shoulder.

"Well," he said, "how would you like me to drive you home, Jerry? I called your mom this morning, and she told me that they had gotten your message that you stayed the night here. I told her that you were safe with us and that I would be getting you home." Jerry's eyes bored into Bill to see if he was being judgmental. He was not. Although neither Bill nor Lori had ever been divorced, they both knew that it was painful for Jerry.

Jerry said that he could walk since it was not very far and thanked Lori and Bill for everything. When Jerry left, Wilhemina just plopped down near the door and whimpered. She could sense his pain.

Since that night, Jerry spent even more time over with the Cranes. Actually, this was a godsend because with Lori's pregnancy, she did not take Wilhelmina out as much anymore. She tired easily, and the doctor told her she should take it easy. In the first months of her pregnancy, by the time Lori closed the shop, it was all she could do to walk up the stairs.

"Jerry," she asked, "we will be needing someone to walk Wilhelmina several times a week. Can you help us out? We will pay you."

This changed as she got further along in her nine months and was able to walk again with Wil, but Jerry kept coming around. Bill enjoyed his company too; it gave him someone to mentor—kind of like an early transition to fatherhood.

ori went down to her shop to get things organized after the Christmas rush. As not to hate Jerry's parents because of how they turned his life upside down, Lori needed to keep busy. She hated them and knew it was wrong because sometimes things happened that could not be changed.

Bill made a few calls. The first call was to his friend John. John was a family lawyer in Seattle. John said that the best thing for Lori and Bill to do is just to be there for Jerry. Bill wished that there was more they could do. Then he called his sister and asked that she try to understand why he and Lori wanted to help Jerry.

"I understand that you both are concerned for him, Bill," Jamie said, but she also knew that it could get sticky, getting involved in someone's family business.

New Year's Day came and went. There were no surprises after that. Lori worked at her shop and Bill at school as normal. They had Jerry as a frequent dinner guest.

Nothing was out of the norm, but they did invite Jerry to come with them during spring break to go to Seattle with them. They were going to see a Mariners' game during spring break.

Lori had some shopping to do to stock up her place before the spring-festival crowd returned. His mom had no problem with it. In fact, she asked, since Jerry was with them, if they could keep him for an extra week. If they did keep him, she could go to Vegas with her boyfriend.

"I mean," Jerry's mom said, "I need this time with Mark so he won't leave me." Bill and Lori could not understand her thinking but said that it would be fine with them for him to stay an extra week.

"I don't understand how any parent cannot see their child first!" Bill exclaimed.

All Lori could do to comfort him was to hug him and pray with him that everything would be all right for Jerry.

It was agreed. They would have him for two weeks.

While in Seattle, they had a great time. Lori got her shopping done in record time because she actually preordered most of it online. She also got to see a new movie that was billed.

That was about all her body would let her do because of her pregnancy though. That gave Bill and Jerry plenty of time together. They went down to the waterfront a couple of times while she was resting and just talked. Bill talked to Jerry about his school.

Next year would be his last year of high school, and Bill wanted to know what Jerry had planned.

"Hey, Jerry, you are quite the photographer. I bet if you wanted, you could turn that into some kind of future," Bill said.

He wondered if he was interested in doing something with the photography that he had done for the yearbook. Photography was just to kill time, said Jerry. He really did not know what he wanted to do and then said that because of the divorce, he did not even know if his parents would have the money to support him if he attended college.

Jerry could not see that far ahead, he said. His mom had been missing work, and they may move to live with her parents. This was not something that he looked forward to, and now more than ever, he just wanted to run away. This talk scared Bill, and he asked him not to make any rash moves.

They got to watch the Mariners win! How exciting it was for Jerry who had not been to a live game before. They were sitting about ten rows behind the catcher, and he forgot about his troublesome world for a few hours. After the game, they retired to their hotel to get rest before heading home to Packwood in the morning.

When they got to Packwood, Wil raced to them.

"She always misses you, you know," Di said. "I know she likes me and doesn't mind my place, but she always runs to you like I beat her." Di went on to say that she wished she had a dog herself.

Di also gave them their mail and said for them to come over and have some tea when they get a chance. They haven't had a chance to catch up in some time.

Wilhelmina always missed them as much as they missed her. Wilhelmina started to form a bond with Jerry too. When Jerry would leave, she would pout. They thought that Jerry would only be with them for the rest of the week, but they received a call from his mom.

She would be living in Las Vegas and wanted him to pack his things because she would be sending for him by June. In the meantime, she arranged for him to stay with her parents.

This made Jerry upset and angry! He yelled at her on the phone and then put his head down and cried. Dropping the phone, he ran to his room and did not even let Wil in. Bill picked up the phone and said they needed to talk.

"Mrs. Hart, Jerry is always welcome here," Bill said. "I will try to get him to call you when he calms down." Temporarily, they decided that Jerry could stay with them.

Lori and Bill felt horrified for Jerry. This was not something that they expected. They knew she was dating someone, but they thought that she would not marry or leave until Jerry graduated. After talking it through with each other, they knocked on Jerry's room. He was lying on the bed, staring up at the ceiling.

Lori stroked his forehead and sat next to him. Bill was standing at the foot of the bed and asked if they could have a serious talk with him. Jerry wiped his eyes and turned his head toward the wall. He was hurting. Bill touched his foot with a light squeeze and said that he and Lori would like to adopt him. Jerry swallowed hard. He loved his mom and dad and wished that all the craziness would stop, but the two people in the world who showed him the most love recently were in this room now.

Another spring festival came along with all the festivities. This year, after the parade, Don's family invited Bill and Lori to his family's home for their first barbecue of the year. Lori decided to close the shop for the day.

"I brought a couple of things for my nephew or niece!" Jamie said and started to unload a truckload of baby items. She already knew the colors of the nursery because Lori and she had been talking about it over the phone and through Skype.

"Oh, Jamie! You do realize that we are only having one child," Lori joked.

They had games, food, and fun. While all the adults ate and watched, the kids played. Later after everyone ate, there was a piñata for the kids to whack. They screamed with glee when it was finally broken open.

There were enough adults and young teenagers to form two teams of softball, and everyone was having a blast. Lori did not participate too much in any of the events because of her pregnancy; however, she did enjoy visiting with everyone. Don and Jamie came from Yakima of course. They stayed at the Lodge as usual but always spent the majority of their time with family.

Their wish was answered in spring. It was not long after the spring festival that Bill and Lori did adopt Jerry. Bill's lawyer friend John made things go smoothly and quietly. They were glad to have adopted him, but they did not think it would be appropriate for him to take their name and let him choose. From that day on, Jerry was known as Jerry Crane.

Because of his age and the fact that his mother just wanted out of Packwood, there were really no problems with the adoption. Jerry's friends started coming around again. His teenage life started growing healthy once more. He began meeting his friends for sodas and even went to a couple of movies with that cheerleader named Kim. He did miss his mother and father a lot, but Lori and Bill gave him a loving environment. Somehow, they knew when he needed space and would ask him to take Wil for a walk so he could gather his senses. Jerry adjusted easily to living with them. Lori and Bill welcomed him with loving arms, and he was a happy extension to their little family.

His high school year ended in June. Jerry helped around with Pleasant Finds. Lori was happy because this late in her pregnancy, she had a hard time getting around. Bill finished his school year also. They were all waiting for Lori to deliver her child.

The happy day came on the twentieth of July. Jennifer Crane was born a healthy, darling eight-pound baby girl to Lori and Bill. The delivery went well without complications, and Lori and Jennifer were home on the twenty-fourth.

It was a beautiful day to come home on; the sun was shining, and it was not too hot. They did not even use the air-conditioning when they drove home. Lori exclaimed when they drove up to the house and saw that there was a large nine-foot stork with a sign stating that it was a girl!

"Leave it to Di," she said. Di had rented one of those hideous yard signs, but how could you not love her for it! Lori was blessed in so many ways through her family and friends. Now a beautiful baby girl increased her circle.

Late-night feedings, running the store, and getting Jerry ready for his senior year were keeping everyone busy. September came fast, and Bill and Jerry were back in the school year.

This year, instead of going on a buying trip, Lori ordered all her purchases online. She would miss getting out on the town, but it was special for her to be spending time with her beautiful daughter. When there were complications on her order, she was quick to get on the phone to find out where the delay in getting her orders was.

Jennifer had her father's light-blue eyes and Lori's fair skin. What a combination; when she gets older, she would be a real beauty. Lori was proud of her new daughter as was Bill.

Don and Jamie came to see their new niece and were just as proud to see how well Jerry had adjusted to his new life! They brought several outfits for Jennifer, a photo album for Lori to fill, and a Seahawk T-shirt for Jerry.

"Jerry, you know you are stuck with us now," said Jamie.

"Don't try to argue with her, Jerry, just accept the love," Don said. "That's what always works for me!"

With his summers off and taking summer courses online, Bill had a lot of spare time to spend with Lori and Jennifer the past summer and loved every moment with them. He especially liked it when they had taken her out on picnics down by the riverside while Wilhelmina ran along the banks, chasing bugs or birds.

When school started, he would have to buckle down and get the band ready; this was the first year they would go on a school trip. There was a band festival for high schools in the surrounding area that was happening in April. He and four other chaperones would be taking his advanced class to Seattle.

School started; this was Jerry's last year. Jerry was now getting used to waking up early for school, and his routine was not interrupted very much by the new arrival of Jennifer. He adored Jennifer as much as her parents did, and each day when he came home from school, he went to her playpen, which Lori placed near her back counter, to give her a kiss.

"How's my little sis?" he would ask and then give her forehead a peck.

Lori and Bill knew that Jerry had not thought of college. He did not want to attend. Bill called his sister Jamie's husband and asked if, at the end of his senior year, Jerry did not change his plans about school, could Bill bring him by. Maybe they could work something out and put Jerry to work there.

"Hey, I mean, if he is interested. That would work out swell because one of my workers would be leaving this fall for college," Don said.

Wow! Many good changes have happened in Bill's life since he had met Lori. After his first wife died, he never thought he could be happy again.

Like every year, the first months fly by, but after Thanksgiving and Christmas, time creeps by, especially for a senior. Jerry was happy one day, and then the next he would be moody because he did not know how to behave with his new freedom fast approaching him. His mother and father called occasionally.

During Christmas, his mother came to Packwood to spend time with her parents and stopped by with a gift for Jerry. She was glad to see Jerry, but anyone could tell they were both hurting inside. She wished that she could have been a better parent, and he wished that he could have his family back. Jerry was happy with the Cranes, but his stomach tightened each time he saw his mom. Lori and Bill gave him space when they saw his need but also gave him more hugs.

When spring came, Bill was busy with getting the band group ready for their trip to Seattle. He had chosen two parents and two teachers to be chaperones. Jerry would not be going—he was not in the band. He and Lori would be driving to Seattle with Jennifer though so they can listen to the final performance. This also allowed Lori to get some shopping done for her shop and to see a play. Lori missed last year's performance and looked forward to going for this one.

Lori had planned to see the play the night after Bill's final performance. Her plan was that when Bill's competition was over, they would have Jennifer stay at the school with all the band students while they attended the play.

The band was not traveling home until the following day anyhow, and the chaperones said it would be fine if he took one night off. This year, *The Producers* was billing. It was a new play, and she was anxious to see it. Both Jamie and Don would be attending with them after they all had a wonderful dinner out on the town.

His band group actually placed. Bill was exuberant; he could not believe that they took first place in the competition—not overall first place but for their performance and for being the most improved. They were a smaller band and did not have all the instruments represented as a larger school would, but they had practiced hard and played better than ever on the night of the competition.

When they received the plaque, he was astounded. Lori and Jerry were in the audience when Bill gave his acceptance speech, and they were clapping and whistling for him as loud as they could. Jennifer bounced on her mother's lap with her finger pointed at her father, saying, "Daddy!"

Before leaving for the play and dinner, Lori ordered a special cake, and they all congratulated each other on their performance. Everyone was happy.

"Thank you all!" Bill said, and his band members began singing "For He's a Jolly Good Fellow," which brought tears to Lori's eyes because she could not agree more.

The students were happy too. Since it was their last night there, the students attended a dance while Bill was out on the town.

When Bill returned from his trip to Seattle, Lori, Jerry, and Jennifer had invited all the band members and their parents for a gathering in their backyard. It was fantastic. The students retold how great it was to receive first place. They had another cake and some soft drinks along with dishes of food that everyone brought. Don and Jamie came too; he grilled hamburgers and hot dogs for everyone.

The school year ended shortly after that. Bill and Lori had Jerry set to go and stay with Jamie and Don. Not before they took their honeymoon though. They decided that they would like it if their whole family could go to Hawaii for a week.

Their whole family included Jennifer, Jerry, *and* their dog. It was fantastic. They stayed at a condominium near the beach. Most nights, they ate in, but one night, they ate out as a family and asked Jerry what he thought about moving to Yakima. Bill told him that his brother-in-law and sister would help him find a place to stay and that they would come and see him often. Jerry agreed that he would like to give it a try and then asked if they would come and visit him.

"As long as you don't make us do the dishes!" Bill said jokingly. It was set.

A week in Maui went fast; they all came back tanned but ready to get back to their normal lives again.

Bill and Lori drove Jerry to Yakima shortly after they got back from Hawaii. Everything went smoothly, and when they left, they were proud of him. Lori was worried about him being alone, so she said that Wil could live with him as long as he brought her back to visit. Jerry was glad to have the company. He thanked and hugged Lori and Bill both, and when they left, he said that he never would have been able to do this if it were not for them.

Although he loved his parents, they were the next best thing, and he said so.

Don took to Jerry right away. He was glad that he did not have any problems that most teenagers had. Jerry was worried that he may let Lori and Bill down. First, Jerry was running the register, and slowly Don gave him other responsibilities. His pay increased when his responsibilities did. He would not be rich anytime soon, but if he managed his money right, Jerry would be able to do well.

As he was unpacking his boxes, he noticed a picture of him and his parents that was taken when he was younger. God, he loved them both, but as he placed that picture for display on his dresser, he noticed a framed photograph of himself with Lori and Bill, his new family. Lori had given it to him before he left. He placed the picture of Bill and Lori next to his parents' picture and felt a tug at his heart. He had found his pleasant finds also and thanked God for his blessings and for bringing Lori and Bill to him.

Jennifer, Jennifer, pretty as a pearl.
She's a little cutie; she's my little girl!